James and Gentletoes

Kenneth Bottomley

First Edition
Copyright © Kenneth Bottomley 2003

All rights reserved. No reproduction, copy or transmission of this publication may be made without written permission. No paragraph of this publication may be reproduced, copied or transmitted save with written permission or in accordance with the provision of the Copyright Act 1956 (as amended).

Author: Kenneth Bottomley
Illustrator: Dominic Parish

This edition published in 2003 by Bottom Line Publishing (1997)

Printed by: Spot On Print & Design
                     Keighley

With thanks to: Dave Clemence   Dave Weeldon
                     Kate Clarke   Geoff Spanton
                     Ian Brooke   Tony Cowham
                     Chris Hardie-Hill

A special thanks to Beryl Dawe without whose help this book would not have been finished.

ISBN 095318041-7
email: Bottom_line_publishing@hotmail.com
Typeset by Visual Reality email: visreal@dsl.pipex.com

For Julie, Emily and Ben

Proceeds from this book will be donated to
The Bradford Royal Infirmary.
Many thanks to all the staff of the children's ward for their loving care
given to our son during his amazing recovery.

CONTENTS

CHAPTER ONE

James is in for a shock

A new school buzzer had just been installed in the hall. Every time it buzzed it was so loud that it nearly made the children jump out of their seats.

This noise meant only one thing to James Marshall – playtime. Time for fun and mischief. He pushed his chair under his desk and raced out of the classroom.

"Last one to the dustbins is a slimy worm!" shouted James.

That's cool thought Ben, one of James' friends as he joined the rest of 4A pushing and jostling out of the school all the way onto the playground.

Mrs. Franks was on playground duty. She was busy looking after a girl called Emily from Reception, who had fallen down the steps.

She nearly fell down again as James, Sarah, Ben, Harlan and Kate scrambled past in their rush to the bins.

"James Marshall! Be careful and look where you are going." Mrs. Franks shouted out. But James couldn't hear, he had flown past with only one thought in his head – to get to the bins.

Children were knocked down and scattered like skittles all over the playground. James got to the dustbins first, banging the lids down with three mighty crashes, "I've won. I am the winner. That was pipsqueak, easy peasy lemon squeezy!"

After getting his breath back, James felt very pleased with himself: that is, until Kate told him he'd just knocked over Adam Jenkins, the school bully, whose dad just happened to be headmaster of Elderston School.

James went as white as a sheet. "No, I didn't push him. It wasn't me. Don't you spread stories about me, Kate."

Adam Jenkins was always playing tricks on James and getting him into trouble - the boys didn't like one another. James knew that Adam would tell his father that it was he who had pushed him to the ground.

The buzzer sounded for the end of playtime.

Back in the classroom Mrs. Salter, James' teacher, spoke sternly to him. "James Marshall, please go and see the headmaster now!"

James stood up and walked away from his desk and out of the classroom without looking at anyone. He muttered to himself. "What can Mr. Jenkins do to me? Keep me in at playtime?

Give me lines?"

He knocked on the headmaster's door.

"Come in" Mr. Jenkins' voice could be heard right along the corridor, sending shivers all the way down James' back.

The headmaster was sitting behind his desk, pen in hand. A muscular man with hairy arms, dark hair, piercing eyes set below bushy eyebrows, he peered at James through specs covering only half his eyes.

"Now boy, what is your name?"

"James, Sir," was the nervous reply.

"Speak up, boy."

"James - Sir!" This time the reply came out like a cannon shot.

No need to shout, boy. Ah, James. Yes, I know you. I remember. The Joker. The Clown. The boy who likes lots and lots of fun. Yes. But pushing people over in the playground isn't very funny. I have your school reports in front of me - now they make grim reading indeed. Do you remember them, James?"

Mr. Jenkins' face appeared to be warming up. "What about the time you tied all the teachers' cars together with the school's tug-of-war rope? It was like a ride on the dodgems. Everybody was bumping into one another. Luckily none of the cars were badly damaged or you wouldn't have been seen here again.

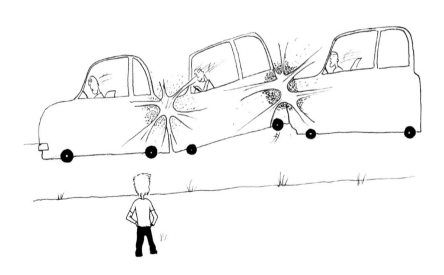

Then there was the time you put superglue on all the chairs in the staffroom!"

James couldn't resist a grin.

"Go on, laugh, laugh! Mrs. Franks didn't laugh. She wasn't at all amused sitting in a bath of soapy water all day to loosen her bottom from the chair.

And what about the school play? Nobody knew who was who with their costumes all mixed up. Superman looked like Batman; Spiderman looked like Robin Hood. I'm lost for words!"

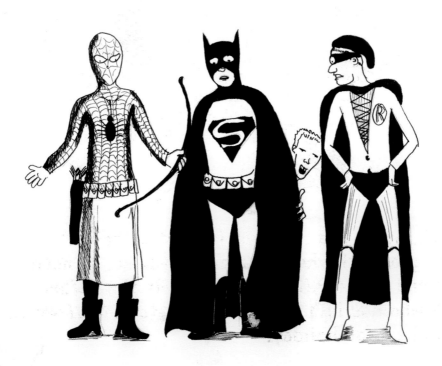

Mr. Jenkins looked directly into James' eyes.

"Well, James Marshall, I've just the cure for you. You do like animals, don't you?"

"Um, yes, Mr. Jenkins, I do," was the cautious reply "I... like... cats and dogs."

"Oh, good. Yes . . . that is what I thought. Very good", the headmaster continued. "I have a friend called Peter who works at the safari park who has left me a small pet to look after while he is on holiday.

It's your lucky day, James, because I am going to let you take it home where you will look after it. You can bring it to school with you every day so that all the other children can enjoy seeing it. But remember . . . it will be your responsibility."

Mr. Jenkins stood up from behind his desk and handed James a sheet of paper. "Here is a list of what it likes to eat and the dos and don'ts of looking after it. Oh, and before I forget, take this licence and this key."

Mr. Jenkins handed James a sealed envelope and fished the key from the drawer of his desk. James put them in his pocket along with the list of instructions. The headmaster reminded James to keep out of trouble and to stop pushing others down in the playground.

"Oh, James, can you ask your Father to come to the school and collect the food. He will need to bring his car."

"This sounds very strange," thought James. "A car to collect food? What sort of animal is this?"

Mr. Jenkins' patience was exhausted. "Go, boy. Just go. You'll find it chained to the school railings behind the gym."

James left the head's office. "Chained? Chained?" thought James. He began to feel hot and sticky and a little sickly.

"What is Mr. Jenkins doing to me? I'm beginning to change my mind about him. I thought he said I wouldn't be punished."

He made his way through the school, passed the gym, and out of the side door leading to the playground.

"Oh, no! What's that?" James leapt back through the open door and slammed it shut! The Head's got to be joking, he thought. My Dad will kill me! He gingerly peeped out just to check that he wasn't imagining things.

CHAPTER TWO

PC Grumpychops makes
a mistake

There it was – a huge wall of enormous grey elephant, with a long trunk, gently swaying from side to side stood before him.

It suddenly spotted James, reached out with its trunk, grabbed him, and lifted him high into the air.

"Put me down!" James shouted. "You great big marshmallow! Now listen to me, you 20 tons of pudding. I'm not frightened of you. Put me down! For the last time, put me down!"

Wonder of wonders! The elephant then placed James down so gently that he could not believe how soft his landing was. There and then James decided to call him Gentletoes.

He unlocked the padlock with the key Mr. Jenkins had given him, released the chain from the elephant's foot, took hold of the tip of Gentletoes'

trunk, and led him across the playground and out of the school gate.

All the children peeped in amazement out of the classroom windows, then very excitedly waved and cheered at James and Gentletoes as they walked hand in trunk up Elderston Road.

A number of folk were out walking. They all politely crossed to the other side of the road. Gentletoes turned his head and with his trunk picked up James, setting him down gently on his broad back.

What a view he had now! He could see into everyone's gardens. "I'm the king of the castle and the boss around here now," thought James to himself.

However, there was another who imagined himself the neighbourhood boss. PC Grumpychops was hiding behind a garden hedge halfway up Elderston Road.

He was watching and waiting for the schoolchildren to come out of school - when they would have fun. PC Grumpychops was very, very, very grumpy and hated to see anyone having fun. The only time he ever smiled was when he was arresting someone.

Suddenly, to his amazement, he spotted an elephant. The next thing he saw was a boy on its back. Just look," he thought. It's James Marshall. I've been trying to catch him for a long time ... he's always playing tricks and having fun." He began to chuckle. "Ha, ha. Goody gumboils! It's my lucky day!"

Out came a walkie-talkie from his trouser pocket. "PC Grumpychops to the Police Station. Escaped elephant on the loose on Elderston Road. Looks like James Marshall has stolen it. Send the Fire Brigade and contact the Safari Park. Over and out."

Gentletoes approached the hedge. Without warning, out sprang PC Grumpychops. "You elephant thief!" he shouted, jumping up and down. A shocked Gentletoes lifted his front legs high into the air, nearly throwing his passenger off, did a full turn, and with James hanging grimly on, charged back down Elderston Road.

PC Grumpychops made chase.

James quickly tweaked Gentletoes' left ear and deftly disappeared up Whackers Lane. PC Grumpychops was given the slip.

As they walked towards James' house the neighbours peeped out from behind the curtains, eyes popping out in disbelief.

Meanwhile back at the Police Station PC Grumpychops was in serious trouble with Inspector Wiseman for wasting Police and Fire Brigade time. There was neither sight nor sound of an elephant. Now even grumpier, he was more determined than ever to get his own back on James Marshall.

Gentletoes was nearly at the Marshall's house. James felt very proud to be riding home from school on the back of his new friend. However, as soon as his Mother saw an elephant with her son riding on top, she fainted!

Fortunately, her fall was somewhat broken by a rhododendron bush. Her neighbour, who was watering his front garden, rushed across with the hosepipe and sprinkled Mrs. Marshall liberally all over.

Now soaked to the skin and mumbling something like, "Wait till your Dad gets home", she went inside the house and slammed the front door very firmly shut.

James just had enough time to chain Gentletoes to the front gate before his Dad came home.

Mr. Marshall was very tired after a long day's work and didn't even notice Gentletoes. He entered the house as usual, asked James if he'd had a good day at school, and gave him a hug.

Peering beyond James and out of the window, his eyes fastened on a gently swaying mass of grey. His hair began to stand on end.

"Where's the circus?" he exclaimed. " I didn't see any circus tents on my way home. Is the elephant keeper talking to Mum?"

"Er, Dad, his name is Gentletoes. He's mine..."

Dad's voice was rising, just as it always did when there was a problem.

"Tell me, James, that this is a joke and you have nothing to do with this elephant."

James' Dad left the room, opened the front door, ran down the garden path, approached Gentletoes and caught hold of his trunk with a sharp tug.

"Come on, Gentletoes, out of our garden."

Gentletoes didn't like his trunk being pulled in such an urgent fashion. James closed his eyes. A long grey trunk curled around Mr. Marshall and he was swiftly despatched across the lawn into the rose bushes.

"Ouch, ouch," cried Mr. Marshall. "Take him away" "But I can't, Dad. I was just about to tell you. It's my punishment for knocking down Adam Jenkins in the playground!"

Mr. Marshall cradled his head in his hands. There was a long, long pause before he reluctantly agreed Gentletoes could stay if he was kept in the garage.

James spent the rest of the evening thoroughly dusting out and tidying up months of jumble, led his new friend to a fresh straw bed and locked him in for the night.

James' Dad went upstairs for a lie down. He said he was suffering from an attack of elephantiasis. His mother sat downstairs crying somewhat hysterically.

However, once everyone had eaten a cheese pizza and enjoyed a nice cup of hot tea, Mr. and Mrs. Marshall agreed that as Gentletoes' food was to be provided and, after all, not everyone had an elephant as a pet, then, provided James looked after him, perhaps it wouldn't be so bad after all.

CHAPTER THREE
The Day of the School Fair

When James woke next morning he couldn't get into the garage quick enough. Gentletoes let out a loud trumpet noise in greeting, put his trunk around James' shoulders and gave him a friendly hug. It was time to go to school.

James carefully chained Gentletoes to the railings. This was a very special day—the day of the School Fair. The children always looked forward to this for weeks beforehand.

There were the usual stalls in the playground - tombola, cake stall, toy stall, coconut shy.

However, the most popular attraction was the throwing of a wet sponge at the various teachers.

James got his sponge as soggy as possible, lifted it high into the air, and putting all his weight behind it

aimed straight at … yes, you've guessed it … Mr. Jenkins! It caught him right between the eyes.

'Well done!" shouted Sarah, jumping up and down in excitement.

Before Sarah had a chance to soak Mr. Jenkins, Gentletoes put his trunk into the big bucket of water and sucked it dry. The contents showered all over the remaining teachers. Oh, dear me! The crowd laughed hysterically — even babies in their prams clapped their hands!

The only ones not laughing were the school staff. They were so wet they had to go inside and get changed, which meant the end of "throw a sponge at teacher."

"It is now time for the tug-of-war. Will all competitors please line up on the school football pitch." Mr. Jenkins' voice boomed out through the school loudspeaker. He sounded a bit cross.

Middleton School was in the next village. Their tug-of-war team had a mascot called Hercules.

"If their mascot is called Hercules, he must be very strong. I have an idea," said James to Ben and Sarah."I'm going to ask the boys and girls if we can use our mascot."

When Middleton discovered Elderston School's mascot was named Gentletoes they immediately agreed — after all, with a name like Gentletoes, they had nothing to be afraid of!

The thick rope was laid in a long line on the football pitch. The teams walked onto the field.

Middleton School lined up at one end, Elderston at the other.

Then the mascots were led on. First came Hercules — a massive lad, more resembling a gorilla than a schoolboy. He already wore size 12 trainers. A great cheer went up from Middleton School. Hercules would easily win the game for them!

James then led Gentletoes onto the field. An enormous gasp went up from the Middleton team. "An elephant" they cried. An elephant called Gentletoes?"

The teams picked up the rope — at one end an elephant, a demoralised Hercules at the other.

"Lift up the rope … take the strain and … pull!" shouted Mr. Jenkins.

Before the word "pull" had gone from his lips, Elderston School had won. Gentletoes just caught the rope round his trunk and pulled. Shocked at the speed and strength of Gentletoes, both teams fell to the ground together.

"Hip, hip, hooray!"

"Hip, hip, hooray!"

"Hip, hip, hooray!" cheered the crowd.

Gentletoes was the hero of the day. James sat on his shoulders and did a lap of honour round the football field, his friend trumpeting all the way.

CHAPTER FOUR
Gentletoes gets James into trouble

The school fair was coming to an end, James and Gentletoes were returning home up Elderston Road. Mayor Munchit's allotment gate was open. After the tug-of-war, Gentletoes was feeling very hungry. It was too late for James to try and close the gate!

"Come out! Come out!" he yelled. "You'll get me in mega trouble!"

To James' surprise, Gentletoes turned around and did as he was told, leaving the juicy vegetables behind - except for an odd leek, three cabbages and a row of peas. James shut the gate tightly and glanced at Mayor Munchit's vegetables.

"Oh, no! No! Just look, Gentletoes at the mess you've made in Mayor Munchit's allotment. I've had it now. I can just imagine what tomorrow's paper will say. JAMES MARSHALL AND A 20 TON MONSTER DESTROY LOCAL MAN'S PRIZE VEGETABLES."

James quickly reached for Gentletoes' trunk and led him away before Mayor Munchit discovered the damage. Mayor Munchit grew famous prize vegetables and entered them in shows all over the country. However, he had a very large appetite and had a tendency to eat much of his produce before it was fully-grown. The schoolchildren made fun of Mayor Munchit.

"Look up there, Mayor Munchit, you haven't eaten that apple."

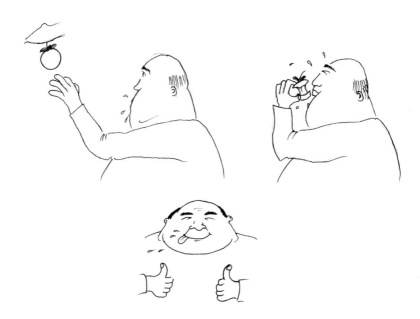

Mayor Munchit rushed to the spot and took an enormous bite. Crunch ... it was gone! He would then lick his lips with a big smile on his face. The children would then run away in hysterics.

A surprise awaited James and Gentletoes when they arrived home. A police car was parked outside the house. Inside sat PC Grumpychops, feeling very pleased with himself. At last he was going to arrest James Marshall. Mayor Munchit had informed the Police Station of his wrecked vegetable plot. PC Grumpychops was mystified until he spotted an important clue. Now he had all the evidence he needed — elephant dung on Mayor Munchit's allotment!

On spotting PC Grumpychops, Gentletoes ran quickly around the back of the house with James following. PC Grumpychops leapt out of his car and went in hot pursuit after them.

"Now then, I've got you now," cried the policeman.

Gentletoes was ready for him, having filled his trunk with the contents of the garden pond. He aimed straight at PC Grumpychops. What a soaking he got!

"Aggghh! Stop it at once," he cried, looking like a drowned rat.

Suddenly Inspector Wiseman and Mr. Jenkins the headmaster appeared round the back of the house. They were shocked to see PC Grumpychops dripping with water.

"You have not been given permission to go swimming," cried the Inspector. "Go home at once and get changed," he added.

"But ... but ... " stammered PC Grumpychops.

"I don't want to hear your excuses. Off you go," replied Inspector Wiseman.

After a pause he spoke sternly to James. 'What is this I hear about Mayor Munchit's allotment? If this is your doing, James, Mayor Munchit is going to prosecute." The Inspector waited for a reply, but James kept silent.

"Come on, James," said Mr. Jenkins. "We know it's you and Gentletoes. You left half a ton of elephant dung on his tomatoes. You'd better sort it out with Mayor Munchit and let's hope it doesn't go to court," continued the headmaster.

Inspector Wiseman and Mr. Jenkins then left.

James made a resolution to keep out of trouble for at least a week.

A few days passed. James was in his bedroom playing with his remote control car when the doorbell rang. His Dad's voice could be heard at the door.

"You'd better come in, Mayor Munchit. He's upstairs. I'll just give him a shout."

James began to feel sick. "Oh, no!" he thought. "He's got me now . . . how can I escape? Ah, I'll just give Gentletoes a call to come over to my bedroom window, then I'll jump onto his shoulders and - whoosh! I'll escape."

But it was too late. His Dad was already in the bedroom telling him to come downstairs.

Mayor Munchit was smiling, licking his lips and holding a huge silver cup. He grabbed James by the shoulders and instead of threatening him said: 'Well done, lad! Look at my splendid silver trophy. I've won the all-England Championship Show. After 25 years of trying, I've grown the largest tomatoes ever

entered -as big as footballs! And it's all thanks to you and Gentletoes. In fact from now on I'd like him to supply me with elephant dung... I'll pay you well."

Mayor Munchit left feeling very happy—he even gave Mr. and Mrs. Marshall some of his enormous vegetables.

CHAPTER FIVE
A Crime is Committed

The following morning James and Gentletoes went to school. As they walked down Elderston Road they heard a shout.

"Hey, James Marshall. You're a big ugly turnip. I'm glad my Dad punished you. You're as daft as that stupid elephant you're sat on."

James looked up. Ah, he should have known. There was Adam Jenkins leaning out of an open bedroom window, grinning like a Cheshire cat.

James didn't have to say a word. Gentletoes leant over into next door's garden and filled his trunk with dirty water from the birdbath.

Raising his trunk high into the air he aimed straight at Adam Jenkins.

Splo-o-o-o-o-sh! The force of the water sent Adam reeling into his bedroom. A loud angry voice followed -it was Adam's Mum.

"Adam, just look at your bedroom carpet, ... it's soaking wet! Where is that water pistol? When I find it you will not see it again."

Adam protested. "It's not me, Mum. It's that silly James Marshall and his elephant."

Mrs. Jenkins did not believe her son; she'd heard too many lies from Adam and thought that this was another of his whoppers.

"Don't tell lies, Adam. It's early to bed tonight and no sweets for a week. This better not happen again."

James laughed all the way to school. When he arrived Mr. Jenkins was waiting at the school gates for him.

"Good morning, James. I would like to thank you for doing such an excellent job of looking after Gentletoes. My friend Peter returns home today from his holiday and will arrive tomorrow to take him back to the safari park."

James only managed to say, "oh!" then turned his face and slowly walked away from Mr. Jenkins. He didn't want him to see the tears already forming in his eyes.

When James arrived in the classroom he was far too upset to speak to any of his friends. The thought occurred to him to run away with Gentletoes but, no, he couldn't leave his Mum and Dad.

When James left school at 4 o'clock he was still very sad. Sarah asked if she could ride home on Gentletoes with him. She thought she could cheer James up. Sarah was very mischievous -both she and James had often planned all manner of pranks.

Big black clouds loomed overhead as they left school. It looked as though there would be a storm. As they rode up Whackers Lane Sarah decided to tell James a joke.

"How is cat food sold?"

I know that one," replied James smiling. So much purr tin."

They both laughed and James began to forget all about Gentletoes returning to the safari park in the morning.

All at once their attention was turned towards old Mrs. Beswick's house, just opposite. A dustbin lid crashed with a terrific din onto the paving flags. They heard the old lady's voice: "Stop, you thieving rascal. Come back here. Help! Help!"

She ran out of her front door and down the path to the garden gate, out of breath and in a very distressed state.

"Did you see that wicked robber," she asked Sarah and James, totally ignoring Gentletoes who stood quietly by.

"No," they both replied. 'We didn't see anybody, honest we didn't, Mrs. Beswick," continued Sarah.

PC Grumpychops suddenly sprang out from

the back of a lilac tree at the bottom of Mrs. Beswick's garden.

He was very angry and hopping about with rage.

"You two idiots … you clod-hopping barbarians … the thief must have heard you and fled. I was hiding behind that tree ready to pounce on him and now you have stopped me arresting him and he has escaped!"

Both James and Sarah felt they hadn't done anything wrong. How were they to know a thief was in Mrs. Beswick's house? If they had known this they would have dived from the top of Gentletoes and squashed him as he came out of the door.

'Well, James Marshall, I'll let you off this time," PC Grumpychops said in his extra-extra grumpy voice, keeping his distance from Gentletoes and remembering what had happened to him the last time they had met!

But an elephant also never forgets. Gentletoes slowly edged his way towards the policeman, trunk raised to give him an almighty smack!

In the nick of time, out of the corner of his eye, PC Grumpychops spotted the long grey trunk heading his way and dived straight over Mrs. Beswick's hedge, landing in some very prickly rose bushes.

"Oh, mother!" shrieked PC Grumpychops. James and Sarah decided not to hang about and with Gentletoes in top gear set off for home.

A red van was parked at the top of the road. Gentletoes headed straight for it, head hung down in a charging position.

James and Sarah couldn't understand what was going on.

"Hey, calm down, Gentletoes. What's wrong?" asked Sarah, in a frightened voice, clinging tightly to James.

"Come on," yelled James. "Jump off!"

Neither of them dared to stay on Gentletoes' back. They had never seen him in this mood before. Standing firmly on the pavement they watched open-mouthed as Gentletoes charged straight at the van, moving it 3 meters up the road. He then pressed the side of his great body against the van, rocking it to and fro.

"Help! Help! Help!" came a terrified voice from inside the van. "Someone save me from this mad monster. Don't eat me! Don't swallow me whole!

Please, someone, help me! Help me! I'll never steal again."

"It's the robber!" exclaimed an astonished James.

"Gentletoes, you are clever," said Sarah, who was now not a bit frightened, only full of admiration for their amazingly clever friend.

"He won't eat you. Don't be so silly," said James.

The two of them were laughing as -guess who? -PC Grumpychops ran up to the van puffing and panting.

"Stop rocking this van, elephant. I'm here now, let me do my job and take this villain away."

He spoke to James. "Clear off – it's about time you were at home. Your mother will be wondering where you are."

James, Sarah and Gentletoes continued slowly on their way home, still smiling at the sight of the terrified robber.

Five minutes after they had left, Inspector Wiseman arrived.

"Well done, PC Grumpychops, that's another one off the streets. I was beginning to have my doubts about you, as I have had a lot of complaints from people in the village about you. They say they don't feel safe with an angry policeman jumping out of bushes all the time. They will have to change their opinion now, though. Well done!"

PC Grumpychops almost smiled. "Thank you, Sir. You've got to have the right approach and I believe in letting them know you mean business. You can't be soft with kids. Be tough with them when they're young and they'll soon know right from wrong."

"Well — er — yes. Hmm! Hmm! Carry on, PC Grumpychops, I'll see your report on my desk tomorrow morning. Goodbye."

The Inspector left. He was still unsure about PC Grumpychops. He was so unpopular and not at all the friendly village bobby he should have been.

The schoolchildren laughed at him and the old ladies nearly died of fright every time he sprang out of the bushes in a rage.

Next day the whole school was talking about the dangerous villain who had robbed Mrs. Beswick and how brave PC Grumpychops had been.

"Fancy getting him into that van and locking the door. I heard that the robber had a huge gun!" said Adam Jenkins.

Emily said that she had heard that the robber also had a razor-sharp knife.

However, Sarah and James knew better. They also knew that PC Grumpychops was not telling the truth.

"Well, what can we do?" Sarah said in a very sad voice. Her face was a picture of disappointment.

James looked at her with a hopeless expression and ran out of the school playground. Mr. Jenkins walked out of his office and approached Sarah.

"Can I have a word?" he said, motioning with his finger. "Sarah, I've just seen James storm out of the school playground. He nearly knocked me over and seemed very upset. Can I be of any help?"

"Well, Mr. Jenkins, we're both very upset. James won't tell anybody the reason why, but I'm going to tell you. It's that grumpy village policeman, PC. Grumpychops."

She then explained to Mr. Jenkins what had really happened the previous night when Robin Houses the robber was caught.

Mr. Jenkins looked surprised and a little shocked at what he heard.

"Right, well thank you for telling me, Sarah. Don't worry any more about it. I'll sort PC Grumpychops out at the presentation later today. Just make sure you and James are there."

James and Sarah were among the crowd, which later gathered in the school playground.

At the very front stood a gleaming silver trophy resting in the middle of Mr. Jenkins' polished dark oak desk. Behind this sat an important looking Inspector Wiseman.

Mrs. Beswick was in her best Sunday navy blue suit next to PC Grumpychops who was looking almost pleased with himself. His mouth formed a faint grin, but his eyes still retained a sly, devious grumpyness about them. After all, once a grumpychops, always a grumpychops.

Mr. Jenkins emerged from the crowd and stood in front of the desk.

"Good afternoon, ladies and gentlemen, boys and girls," he bellowed in his authoritative voice.

"Thank you for coming today. As you know, we are here this afternoon to present this magnificent trophy in appreciation for the capture of Robin Houses. We now feel safer in our homes and are grateful that Mrs. Beswick came to no harm. I shall now ask the Inspector to present the trophy to our three unknown heroes."

PC Grumpychops immediately stood up and started to make his way to the front of the desk. He had been so excited about receiving the trophy that he had not heard about the "unknown heroes."

Inspector Wiseman was the next to speak.

"Could James Marshall, Sarah Johnson and Gentletoes please make their way to the front."

There followed a big round of applause.

On hearing and seeing this, PC Grumpychops went a most peculiar shade of purple. Then his face drained and changed to white! Gentletoes came closer. The policeman was gripped with fear as their eyes met.

"Aaaaagh! Don't let that elephant near me. I'm sorry. I'm sorry, I didn't mean to lie."

PC Grumpychops hastily dived under the desk, helped on his way by a gentle tap from Gentletoes.

Inspector Wiseman continued. "It gives me great pleasure to award this special bravery award to Sarah, James and Gentletoes. I also have some good news. Gentletoes is going back to the Safari Park tomorrow morning. Mr. Jenkin's friend, Peter, has returned from his holiday and I have spoken to him on the telephone."

"That isn't good news," said James. It is very sad! I shall miss Gentletoes very much. He has become a special friend to me."

"Ah, yes, I know, James," replied Mr. Jenkins. "But the good news is that you can visit Gentletoes whenever you wish. And the best thing of all is that every Friday at 1 o'clock, Peter is going to bring Gentletoes to the school for you to look after until teatime."

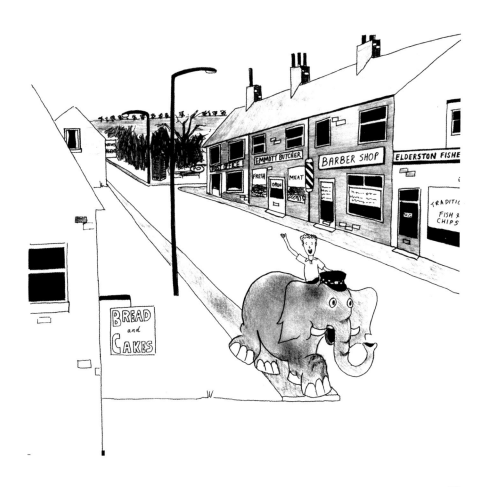

"During this time, James, the people of Elderston have made a special request -they would like you to ride around the village on Gentletoes and check that it is safe and crime-free."

A huge cheer for Gentletoes came from the crowd. James was so excited he nearly burst!

"Three cheers for Gentletoes,", cried Major Munchit, who would now have a continuous supply of elephant dung for his prize vegetables! "Hip, hip, hooray!" "Hip, hip, hooray!" everyone shouted.

PC Grumpychops was sent back to the Police Academy. He will have to learn how to be a friendly village policeman. Perhaps Gentletoes, James and Sarah will go and visit him sometime.

THE END

I would be delighted to hear your comments on the story and pictures in this book. Please write to:

Mr. K. Bottomley
20 Barden Drive
Eldwick
Bingley BD16 3PH
West Yorks.